Having Fun

Then and Now

Lara Whitehead

Harcourt Achieve

Rigby • Steck-Vaughn

www.HarcourtAchieve.com
1.800.531.5015

PM Extensions Nonfiction
Ruby

U.S. Edition © 2013 HMH Supplemental Publishers
10801 N. MoPac Expressway
Building #3
Austin, TX 78759
www.hmhsupplemental.com

Text © 2003 Cengage Learning Australia Pty Limited
Illustrations © 2003 Cengage Learning Australia Pty Limited
Originally published in Australia by Cengage Learning Australia

4 5 6 7 8   1957   14 13
4500435530

Text: Lara Whitehead
Printed in China by 1010 Printing International Ltd

Acknowledgments
The author and publisher would like to acknowledge permission to reproduce material from the following sources:
AAA Collection, p. 19B;AAP Image, p. 22 & bottom, p. 31 bottom left /Thomas Kienzle, p. 6 /POOL, p. 7 /Walt Disney/Joan Marcus, p. 11 /Jeff Walker/Famous, p. 23 top /Dean Lewis, p 23 bottom; Australian Picture Library/Corbis/Michael Nicholson, back cover, p. 20 bottom /Adam Wollfitt, p. 13 top /Historical Picture Achieve, p. 19D; Bridgeman Art Library/LaurosGiraudon, pp.18 (Deck of Cards), 19E; Corbis, p. 20 top;photolibrary.com, pp. 8, 13 bottom, 17, 18 (Dice, Checkers), pp. 26-27, 29 bottom, 31 top right; Picture Desk/ArtAchieve, p. 12 /Musee du Lourve/Dagli Orti, p. 5 top /Egyptian Museum Caior/Dagli Orti, p. 19C/National Museum Karachi/Dagli Orti, p. 19F /Bettmannm pp. 24, 31 top left /Bargello Museum Florence/Dagli Orti, p.30 bottoml Stock Photos, pp. 4-5 bottom, 28 /Masterfile, front cover, p. 29 top.

Having Fun, Then and Now
ISBN 978 0 75 789239 4

Contents

Chapter 1

Sports

Playing and watching sports has been a form of entertainment for thousands of years. The ancient Greeks started the Olympic Games, while the Romans built huge stadiums to watch chariot races. Today millions of people still play or watch sporting events for fun.

The ancient Olympics

Almost 2,800 years ago, the first ancient Olympic Games were held in Greece. They were part of a religious festival in honor of Zeus, the father of all the Greek gods and goddesses. The only event held in the very early Olympic Games was the foot race.

A modern stadium can hold hundreds of thousands of spectators.

Art showing an athlete arriving at the Olympic Games 1,500 years ago

The word **athlete** comes from an ancient Greek word that means "one who competes for a prize." At the ancient Olympic Games, the greatest prize for winners was a branch from a wild olive tree, but there were other prizes, too.

Some champions received a lifelong prize from their **city-state.** If you were a champion from Athens, you might have been awarded one free meal a day at the city hall for the rest of your life. Or you might have been allowed to live free of charge in the **Pyrtaneum**, a special hall where important citizens lived. Other city-states allowed champions to stop paying taxes for four years. Other ancient prizes for Olympic champions included oxen, shields, woolen cloaks, and olive oil.

The modern Olympics

Today the Olympic Games include many different sports, such as ice skating, mountain biking, softball, and gymnastics. Millions of people around the world watch them on television. However, unlike athletes in the past, modern athletes compete for gold, silver, and bronze medals.

Katharine Merry (Great Britain), Cathy Freeman (Australia), and Lorraine Graham (Jamaica) display their 400 metres medals at the 2000 Olympic Games.

The modern Olympics also include other forms of entertainment. Opening ceremonies – such as those at the 2000 Olympic Games in Sydney, Australia – blend music, dance, and theater. At the end of Sydney's opening ceremony, athlete Cathy Freeman lit the Olympic flame in a dramatic ending to the night's entertainment.

Cathy Freeman lighting the Olympic flame at the 2000
Olympic Games in Sydney, Australia.

Chapter 2

The London Times July 10, 159

THEATER

Romeo & Juliet

a play by Shakespeare

Reviewed by Matthew Inkspot

Last night was the opening of a new play by William Shakespeare, called *Romeo and Juliet*. Romeo and Juliet fall in love, but their families hate each other. They refuse to allow the two young people to see each other. If you want to know how the story ends, come to the Globe Theater this weekend.

Admit One
Romeo & Juliet
one penny

The best actor was the young boy who played Juliet. Since no women were allowed on stage, boys played all of the female parts. They looked quite lovely in their dresses and wigs!

Unfortunately the special effects in the play were rather basic. Romeo carried a burning torch when it was supposed to be night time. Juliet's balcony was just a small platform above the stage. However, the words were so beautiful that I could still imagine Romeo in a lush garden, wooing Juliet on her stone balcony.

You can buy a ticket to the play for just one penny, but you'll have to stand on the dirt floor of the pit below the stage. Three pennies will get you to the Gentlemen's Room with a cushion for the hard wooden benches. Wealthy viewers might wish to pay more and sit in the upper levels of the theater. When the trumpet blasts, be sure to quiet down so the play can begin.

Overall I think *Romeo and Juliet* is a rather good play and worth the ticket price. Let's hope Shakespeare continues to write more plays in the future.

My First School Play

by Tanisha, Grade 4

Last weekend I was in my first play at school. We had to practice a lot after school. All the fourth grade kids turned into great actors. On opening night, my mom and dad came to see me perform. Some actors wore painted masks with glitter. Others wore clothes in bright colors. Sam and William carried props in the first act. Most of us sang and danced on stage, too. I was so happy all the kids remembered their lines. Everyone had so much energy!

At the end of the show, the school band marched on stage. Lights flashed. Streamers fell onto the stage. Parents cheered and clapped.

I loved singing, dancing, and learning my lines. Acting takes a lot of practice, but sharing my talent on stage was so much fun!

The stage

The basic design for theaters hasn't really changed since ancient times. But modern theaters do have some extra features, such as fancy lighting and staging equipment, comfortable seating, speaker systems, and the orchestra pit.

This amphitheater was built in Ostia, Italy during the time of the Roman Empire.

A curved seating plan, set on a slope, allows many people to see the entire stage at the same time.

This model shows how the theater would have looked in 1599.

In Shakespeare's Globe Theater, the cheapest tickets let you stand directly in front of the stage.

In modern theaters, seats directly in front of the stage are often the most expensive.

Chapter 3

Home

Snowed in at Grace's house

February 20, 1880

Dear Diary,

Today it snowed for the third day in a row. The sno[w]
too deep for us to play outside. So we played together i[n]
Yesterday the Kellors came to visit in their sleigh and st[ayed]
overnight. This morning Klara and I cut out paper dolls [from]
bits of newspaper. David and Eli played checkers. Then [?]
jumped onto the board and knocked all of the pieces o[n the]
floor! One of the black pieces got lost. Father made a [?]
the afternoon.

Mr. Kellor also brought his **fiddle** and we sang toge[ther]
dinner cooked. After dinner we had a square dance! I[t was]
great fun!

Mr. Kellor started off playing slowly while we practiced. Then he began to play faster and faster, so we had to dance faster and faster. Afterwards we all laughed and sat down by the fire to rest.

Father brought out the corn popper, and we ate popped corn while Mrs. Kellor told us stories about her childhood. When she was a little girl, her family moved from Pennsylvania to Oregon in a covered wagon. I'd heard her story before, but I always like hearing it again.

Now it's time to blow out the candle. I hope the snow will stop tomorrow so we can go sledding outside. Klara and I plan to make the biggest snowman ever!

Goodnight!

Grace

E-mail from Zara

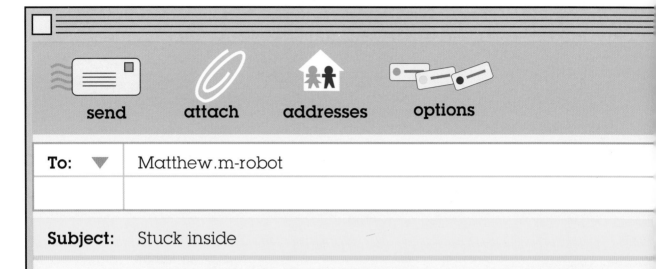

send   attach   addresses   options

To: ▼   Matthew.m-robot

Subject: Stuck inside

To: Matthew in Australia
From: Zara in London
Re: Stuck inside

Hi Matthew,

We're having a heatwave and I'm stuck inside today. It's 109°F outside and Mom says we're staying out of the sun until after 3:00 at least. I've been playing computer games this morning, but I'm kind of sick of them now.

How are you doing with building your robot? I've got mine so he moves his head, but I can't make his arms move with the remote yet. I think one of the wires must be loose, but I can't figure out which one. I'll e-mail you a video clip when I get him working.

Have you got your new digital camera yet? Send me a photo of the snow at your house. I could make it my screen saver and pretend it's cold in my house when I see it!

I've got to go and turn down the air conditioner. Mom will have a fit if she notices how cold I set it!

Talk to you soon,

Zara

Mix and match

Today we have many types of games to play, but some of them were invented long ago. Can you match the old games to the new ones?

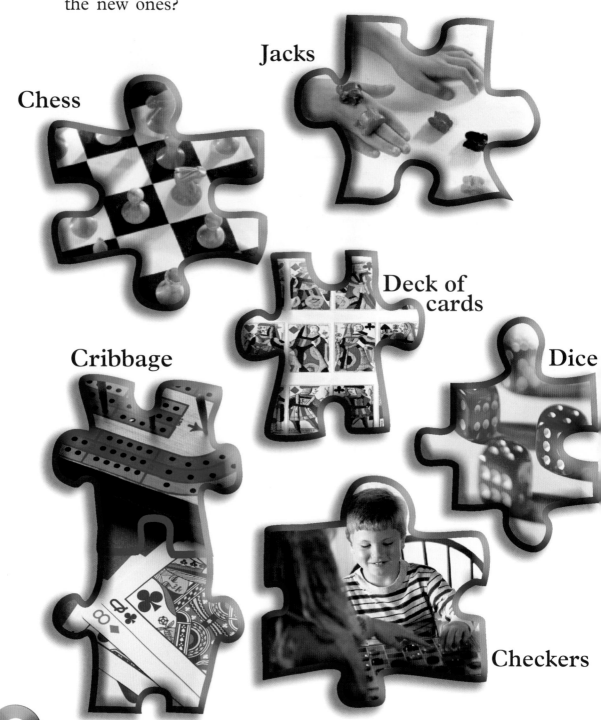

Jacks

Chess

Deck of cards

Cribbage

Dice

Checkers

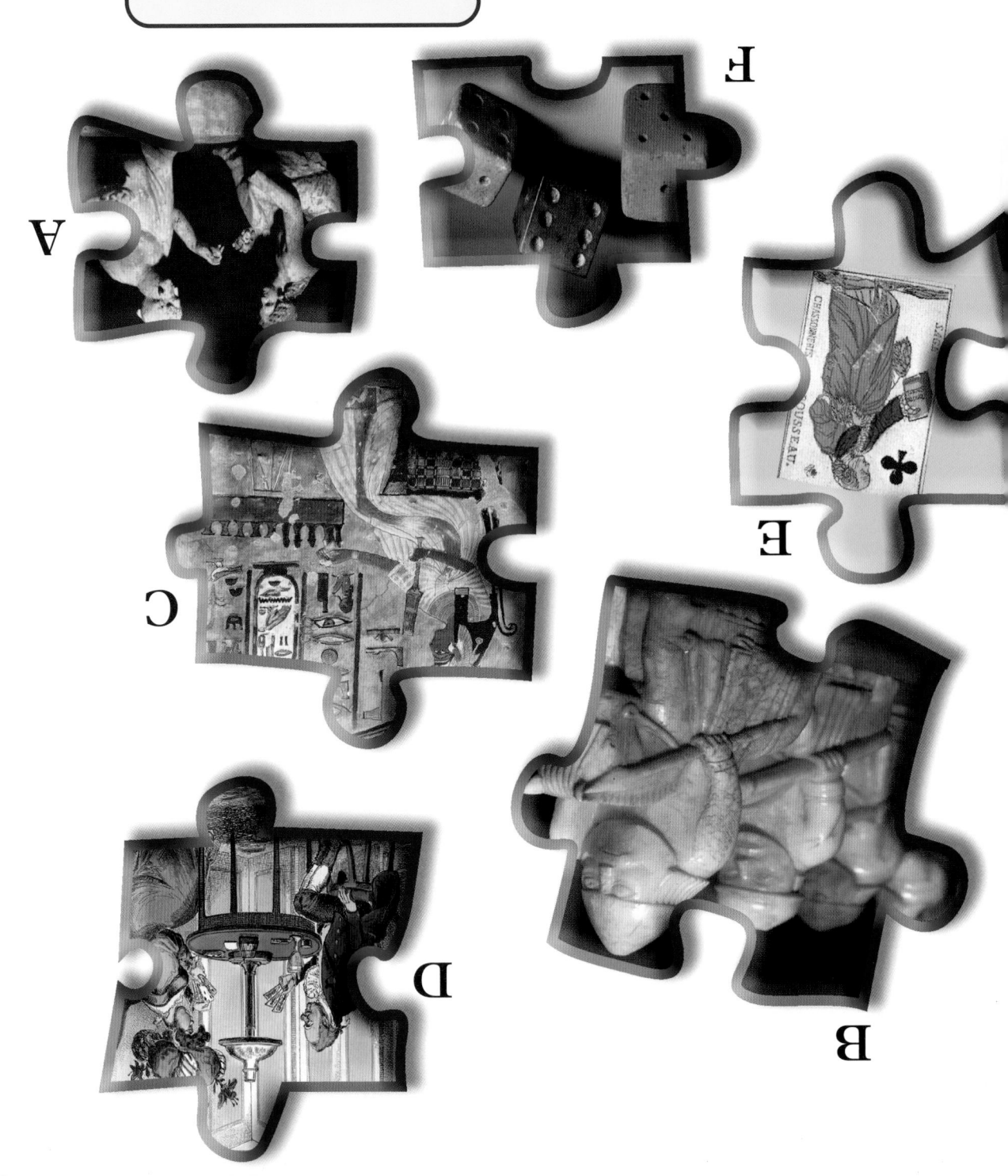

19

Answers:
A Jacks, 2,000+ years ago
B Chess, 800+ years ago
C Checkers, 3,300+ years ago
D Cribbage, 1800s
E Deck of cards, 1793
F Dice, 4,500+ years ago

Chapter 4

Music

Minstrels

Around 800 years ago, wandering musicians called minstrels
started traveling from town to town across Europe. They
entertained peasants and kings, singing songs of love, war, and
brave deeds. They played instruments like the harp, the recorder,
and the lute.

Come One, Come All
to an
Evening's Entertainment
by
The Traveling Minstrels of Paris

Hear them sing their famous songs:

Hopeless Love for a Noble Lady

Searching, Searching for a Unicorn

And, winner of the French Court's

Most Popular Song of the Year,

She Loves Me, She Loves Me Not

One show only!

Also featuring juggling and acrobatics!

See them tonight

at The Lute in Arms, Baker's Street

The Beatles wave as they arrive at London airport, England.

Beatlemania!

In the early 1960s, a British band called The Beatles hit the charts with their song, Love Me Do. They soon became the most famous pop group in history. During their time together, The Beatles traveled to many countries to play their music.

People around the world could hear their songs on the radio, buy their record albums, go to concerts, and even see them on TV or in the movies. For one of the first times in history, radio, and TV allowed millions of people to enjoy the same music at the same time.

Today there are lots of music groups that are famous around the world. Their songs travel much more quickly these days. We can watch **webcasts** of concerts and listen to music on CDs and DVDs.

Chapter 5

Machines

Riding high in the sky

Ferris wheels were invented more than a hundred years ago, but they have not changed very much in that time. The first Ferris wheel was built by a bridge builder named George Ferris. He designed his amusement ride for the Chicago World's Columbian Exposition of 1893, in Illinois. Four years earlier, the Paris Expo (in France) had built the Eiffel Tower. The Chicago Expo wanted something even bigger and better.

Interview with Mr. George Ferris, inventor of the first Ferris wheel.

Reporter: What made you decide to build a giant wheel?

Mr. Ferris: The Chicago Expo wanted something really amazing for people to come and see. I always thought that merry-go-rounds were fun, so I decided to build a huge one, only I turned it on its side. That's how I came up with my giant wheel idea.

Reporter: How big is your wheel?

Mr. Ferris: It's 246 feet tall, and can hold 2,160 passengers. It's the biggest wheel in America today.

Reporter: How did you actually build the wheel?

Mr. Ferris: We hired the Detroit Bridge and Iron Works to make the wheel. They were a little surprised when they saw the plans, though! They thought I was just nuts to build a wheel that big.

Reporter: And when the Expo is finished, what will happen to your wheel?

Mr. Ferris: Well, it's just going to get cut up and sold for scrap metal. I don't think anyone will ever build one again. Too bad – I thought it was a fun idea.

The London Eye

If you thought Ferris wheels were an old-fashioned ride, you should see the new London Eye in England! It's twice as tall as Mr. Ferris's wheel.

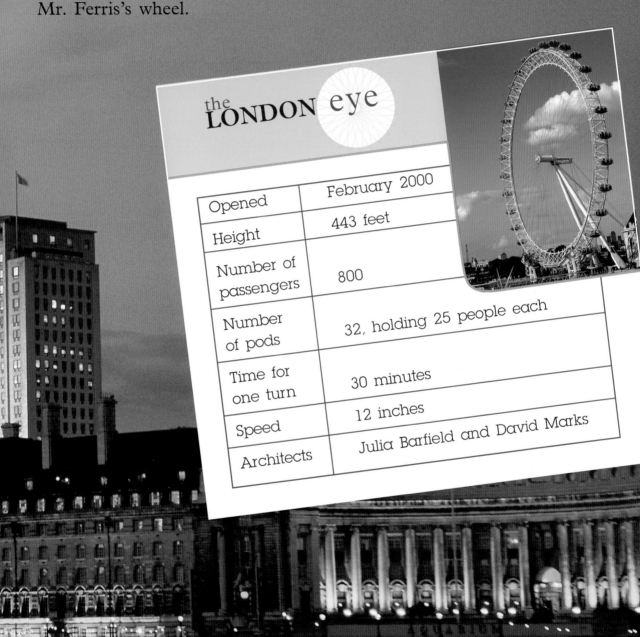

the LONDON eye

Opened	February 2000
Height	443 feet
Number of passengers	800
Number of pods	32, holding 25 people each
Time for one turn	30 minutes
Speed	12 inches
Architects	Julia Barfield and David Marks

Chapter 6

Changing Technology

Technology has changed the way we enjoy lots of types of entertainment, but it hasn't really changed the things we still like to do:

• Sports fans can watch slow-motion instant replays

• Video replays also help sporting officials make calls during a game

• CDs and DVDs mean we can listen to music in comfort, or on the move

- The internet allows us to play computer games with people from around the world

- Hand-held computer games mean we can take our entertainment with us

- Musicals and plays on stage use computer lighting and lasers to add special effects to the show

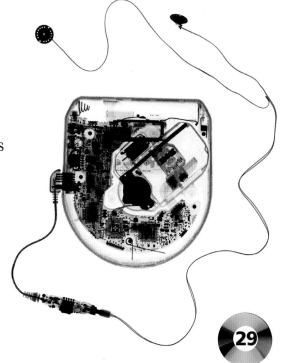

Chapter 7

Timeline

3,400 years ago

People start to play checkers

2,800 years ago

The first Olympic Games are held

2,600 years ago

First written mention of chess

1200

Wandering musicians, called minstrels, appear in France

1300

The first playing cards are mass produced in Europe

1600s

The rules for cribbage appear written down

1592

Shakespeare writes *Romeo and Juliet*

Admit One
Romeo & Juliet
one penny

1893

First Ferris Wheel built at the World's Columbian Exposition of Chicago

2000

The London Eye opens

1939

First television broadcasts are made

1980s

Music CDs become available

1975

The home version of *Pong*, one of the first video games, is released

1960s

The Beatles become popular

1972

The first home VCR becomes available

Glossary

athlete	a person who competes in a sport
chariot	a racing cart with two wheels, pulled by a horse
city-state	a state made up of a city and its surrounding towns
festival	a time of celebration
fiddle	violin
minstrels	wandering musicians in France
Pyrtaneum	a special hall where important citizens lived
webcasts	video recordings played over the Internet
Zeus	the father of all the Greek gods and goddesses

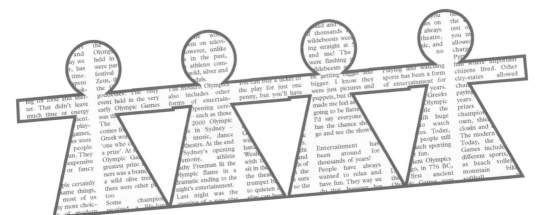